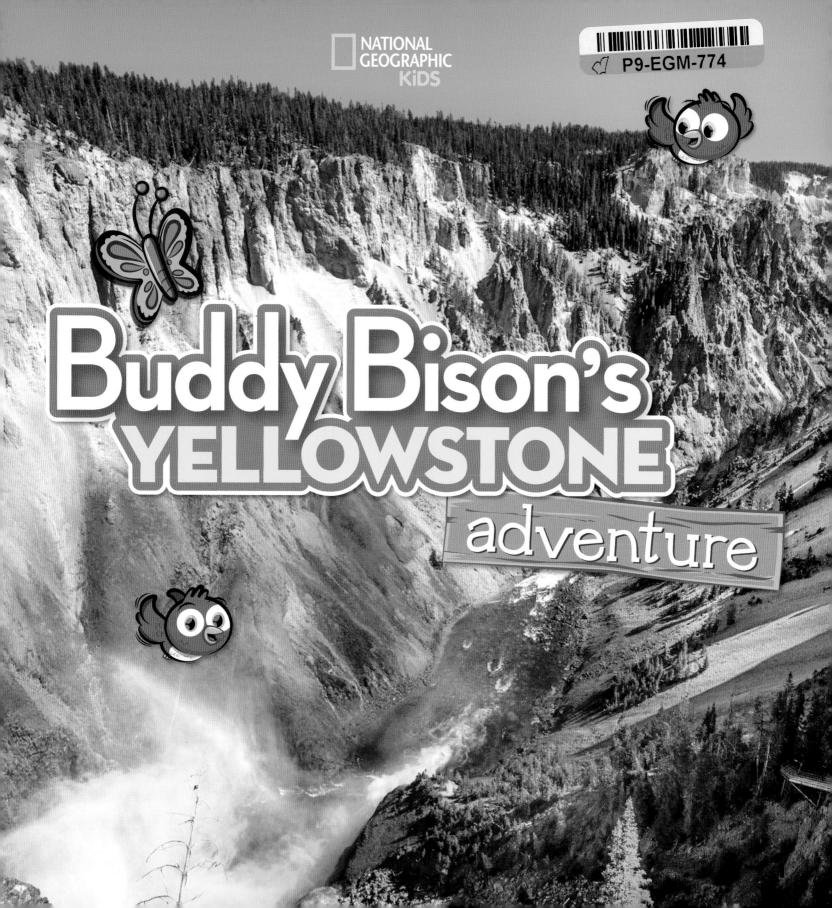

NATIONAL GEOGRAPHIC KiDS

P9-EGM-774

Buddy Bison's YELLOWSTONE adventure

NATIONAL
GEOGRAPHIC
KiDS

Buddy Bison's
YELLOWSTONE
adventure

ILONA E. HOLLAND

NATIONAL GEOGRAPHIC
WASHINGTON, D.C.

INTRODUCTION

One of my fondest memories is of a road trip I took many years ago with a dear friend. We traveled from Alaska all the way to Washington, D.C. That trip across the country took me through many beautiful national parks.

In my 60-year career at the National Geographic Society, my singlemost important mission was to get our youngest readers interested in geography and the world. My work took me all across the globe, but I never forgot how privileged we are to have so many wonderful parks close to home.

2016 marks the 100th anniversary of the National Park Service, and looking forward, we hope the next 100 years see a continued commitment to getting families and their larger communities involved with their parks. Parks are wonderful resources for outdoor education, fitness, recreation, resurrecting the human spirit, and best of all, making lifelong memories.

For thousands of kids across the country, **Buddy Bison** serves as a mascot and a reminder of the extraordinary adventures waiting for us all in parks. He also helps teach the importance of being conscientious park visitors and future park stewards. *Buddy Bison's Yellowstone Adventure* is a unique opportunity for the earliest readers to learn more about all that parks have to offer as together we promote the long-term success of our wonderful parks programs.

I hope your family gets inspired to explore your local, state, and national parks—and be sure to bring Buddy Bison with you! In the words of Buddy Bison, I invite you and your entire family to "Explore outdoors, the parks are yours!"

Gilbert Grosvenor
Chairman Emeritus, National Geographic Society

Buddy Bison® is the beloved mascot for the National Park Trust.

"HEADS!" Christopher yelled, from the backseat.

His favorite nickel landed next to him, bison side up. "Yes!" Christopher whooped. "That means we get to see bison today."

"Actually, it means your twin sister gets to choose what we do on my day off," Aunt Rosa said.

Christopher's shoulders sagged. "OK, you're the park ranger," he said, sighing.

"Hot springs!" Elena exclaimed. "I heard there are millions of microbes there."

"You got it," Rosa said pulling onto the road.

"No," said Aunt Rosa slowing down. "That's steam escaping from a vent in the ground. We are in a hydrothermal area."

"Fire?" Elena heard a worried voice rise from her backpack.

"Buddy, shhh," she whispered as she reached down to put her fingers over the small soft bison clipped to her pack.

"What did you say?" asked Christopher, pointing his camera at the steam.

Elena shrugged.

"Look at this view ..." Rosa was interrupted by the sharp crackle of her radio.

"Ranger Rosa, hikers reported sighting injured birds near CRACK! CRACK! the trailhead of Grand Prismatic Spring. CRACK! CRACK! How soon can you be there?"

"Ten minutes."

"I hope the birds will be OK," said Elena.

"Me, too. I'm glad the hikers called. Visitors should never handle wildlife in the park," Rosa added.

Elena poked Christopher in the side. "That goes for bison," she said.

"Not funny," Christopher replied, shoving the bison coin into his pocket. "Is Grand whatchamacallit a hot spring?"

"You bet," Rosa answered.

"**You two** start looking for injured birds," Rosa said. "I will ask the hikers if they have seen or heard anything."

Christopher grabbed his camera. Elena set down her backpack and hunched over the bushes searching for signs of fallen birds. She looked beneath the low branches.

"Christopher," she said as she straightened, "do you think we are looking in the right place?" There was no answer. "Christopher?"

Christopher was gone.

As Elena looked around, she saw a massive bison staring down at her.

14

Buddy was no longer a small soft toy on her backpack. He was alive. And huge!

"You're here!" Elena squealed as she hugged him. "Where's Christopher?"

"I don't know," Buddy sighed.

"He's going to be in so much trouble," Elena replied. "Help me find him before he gets lost. This park is enormous!"

"Yeah, 3,000 square miles," Buddy said. "It's got lots of geysers like Old Faithful, and this is the only park where bison can roam wherever they want. I love this place!"

"Buddy, not now," Elena interrupted, "we have to find Christopher!"

Suddenly something screeched in the distance.

"What's that?" asked Elena. "Do you think it's one of the injured birds?"

"It sounds more like a person," said Buddy. "It could be Christopher." Buddy took off in the direction of the strange sound.

"Hey, wait!" cried Elena as she started to run. "Remember only bison can run 35 miles an hour."

Elena lagged far behind. "Is he up ahead?" she shouted.

Buddy stood very still and waited for Elena to catch up.

"**No,** he's not here," said Buddy. "But, I can hear him. The sound is coming from that direction." Buddy threw his massive head to the left. "If he keeps making noise, we can find him."

Elena's eyes filled with tears.

Buddy gave her a gentle nudge. "Watch your step and keep searching."

After a few more minutes, Buddy called out. "I see him."

"Where? Is he OK? "

"I think so," Buddy snorted, "but I can't tell for sure. He seems to be hopping around."

Through the trees, Elena saw Christopher waving his hands wildly in the air.

"Hurry! You've got to see this!" Christopher called.

By the time Elena reached her brother, she realized he had found something amazing. The twins stood together gazing out over the thermal spring.

"Look at those colors!" Christopher grabbed Elena's arm. "It's like aliens built this hot spring. I've taken tons of pictures."

"There aren't any aliens," Elena scolded, pulling away. "Pictures? Don't you know how much you scared us?"

"Ahem," Buddy grunted.

When Elena turned, Buddy had disappeared.

"I thought I might see bison from over here," Christopher explained, "but no luck." Elena hid a small smile.

"You know the rules," she huffed. "Aunt Rosa is going to be really mad."

"Not if we get back right away," Christopher said. "Race you!"

When they reached the van, Rosa was waiting. "You know you are never supposed to go off without asking me. I could barely see you."

"We're sorry," they said together. "We won't do it again."

"Did you find the birds?" Elena asked, catching her breath.

"Actually we did, and they were OK. Let's go follow the boardwalk around Grand Prismatic Spring."

"I hear it's like walking on Mars," Christopher winked at Elena.

As they left the hot springs, Christopher shouted. "Look!"

He found it hard to hold still as he aimed his camera. "There they are! BISON!!"

"You never know about bison," Elena smiled. It seems they can show up anywhere."

♡ Elena's Journal ♡

June 21

Today was great! We saw Grand Prismatic Spring, the largest spring in Yellowstone! In fact it is the third largest hot spring in the WHOLE world. The spring is created because gallons and gallons of hot water bubble up through the rocks below. A park sign said that 560 gallons enter the spring every 60 seconds. That's enough to fill a whole fire truck in a minute.

The entire place is steaming hot. No wonder! The water temperature is between 147° and 188°F. Aunt Rosa said my bath water is usually about 95°F. That means the spring is almost twice as hot. YOW!!!

Blue! Red! Yellow! The colors are awesome! Since the center of the spring is the hottest, almost nothing can live there. That's why it is such a clear, deep blue. As the water flows to the edges, it cools. Different algae, bacteria, and microbes live at each of the different cooler temperatures. We can't see them, but they make circles of bright color. These creatures are called thermophiles, or tiny living things that love heat.

Christopher spent most of the day with his head glued to his camera. All he ever wants to do is take pictures. Maybe if he weren't so interested in pictures, he wouldn't have gotten us in trouble for wandering off and not telling our aunt! It's a good thing Buddy helped me find him. I don't know what I would do without Buddy.

BIG S-E-C-R-E-T: Buddy only talks to me. He is the best bison in the whole world!!! He is my BFF.

At the end of the day, we saw lots of big bison. I mean 6 feet tall and between 1,000 and 2,000 pounds big. At that size, it's no wonder they are the largest land animals in North America. I think they are AMAZING!!!

Wow! Grand Prismatic Spring

Geysers spray really high!

Buddy relaxing by Old Faithful

Bison can be anywhere.

Be sure to stay on the path!

Bison are huge!

How deep is this?

That's HOT water!

Bison crossing sign at hot springs

CHRISTOPHER'S PICTURES JUNE 21

BUDDY'S STUDY

WORD OF THE DAY: bellow
The word "bellow" means to make a deep loud sound. Bison bellow. Their grunts and roars can be heard up to three miles away on a quiet day. How loud can you yell?

TO ANSWER YOUR QUESTION
What's the difference between a bison and a buffalo? The answer is that there is no difference. The name bison is more scientifically correct, though. That's why I'm called Buddy Bison.

FAVORITE SPOT
I am not alone! There are more bison (about 4,000) in Yellowstone National Park than anywhere else in the U.S.A. I can always find another bison here.

27

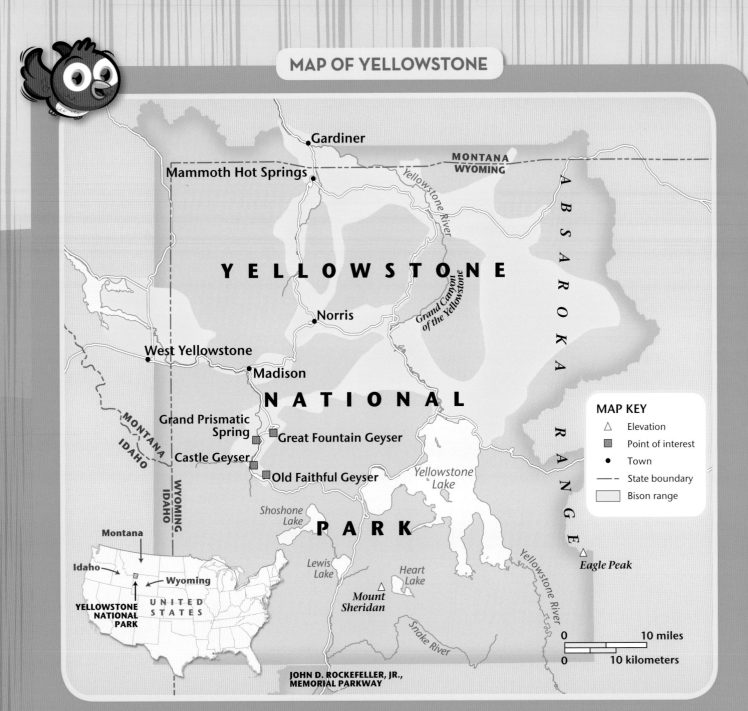

Gardiner

MONTANA
WYOMING

Mammoth Hot Springs

Yellowstone River

Y E L L O W S T O N E

A B S A R O K A

Grand Canyon
of the Yellowstone

Norris

N A T I O N A L

West Yellowstone

Madison

Grand Prismatic
Spring

Great Fountain Geyser

Castle Geyser

Old Faithful Geyser

MONTANA
IDAHO

WYOMING
IDAHO

Yellowstone
Lake

MAP KEY

△ Elevation

■ Point of interest

● Town

- - - State boundary

Bison range

Shoshone
Lake

P A R K

R A N G E

Lewis
Lake

Heart
Lake

Yellowstone River

△ Eagle Peak

Montana

Idaho

Wyoming

△
Mount
Sheridan

UNITED
STATES

YELLOWSTONE
NATIONAL
PARK

Snake River

0   10 miles

0   10 kilometers

JOHN D. ROCKEFELLER, JR.,
MEMORIAL PARKWAY

Yellowstone is a very large park. It is so large that it has parts
in three different states: **WYOMING, MONTANA, AND IDAHO.**

HISTORY OF YELLOWSTONE

Yellowstone began when a giant volcano exploded. It blew not once but several times over the last two million years. Each explosion changed the land. The last eruption, **174,000 years ago,** created the West Thumb of Yellowstone Lake. Today, the park still sits high on top of Yellowstone Volcano.

The lava that flowed from the volcano cooled quickly. It created lots of black rock called obsidian. After thousands of years, **American Indians** came to live in the area. The obsidian rock was perfect for making arrowheads. It was sharp and light. The American Indians used arrowheads and other tools to fish and hunt the wildlife, including the bison, for food. They used the furs for clothing and shelter.

In the 1800s explorers and trappers discovered Yellowstone. They told stories of the unusual landscape. They described the **steam coming out of the Earth** and the beautiful strange colors of the springs. Soon crowds came to see for themselves. But people got greedy. They started trapping animals for their furs. They cut down trees and began mining. The future of Yellowstone was in danger!

President Ulysses Grant wanted to protect the land and animals. Creating a national park was a new idea. On March 1, 1872, Yellowstone became the **first national park in the world!**

Today, Yellowstone is one of America's most popular national parks. More than three million people visit each year. Yellowstone Volcano still bubbles under the earth. It heats the water for **Grand Prismatic Spring** and for Old Faithful, a famous geyser. Old Faithful sends 8,400 gallons (32,000 L) of boiling water high into the air 17 times each day. People come from all over the world to see the natural wonders of Yellowstone. **MAYBE ONE DAY YOU CAN VISIT, TOO.**

5 TIPS ON PARK PRESERVATION

1 **Always stay on marked paths and boardwalks.** Plant life and thermophiles are fragile. Your footsteps could damage them, and hot springs can burn you!

2 **Never touch or feed any wild animal,** not even the squirrels. If you see a hurt animal, let a ranger know. Don't try to help the animal yourself. Always keep your distance. The animals you see are wild.

3 **Put ALL trash and food in bear-proof containers.** Bears are good at finding trash that could make them sick.

4 **Never take any plants, rocks, or creatures** from the parks. Take photos and your stories.

5 **Stop.** Take a long look around— all the way around. Enjoy and appreciate the beauty of the open spaces at the park. Listen for the sounds of water or birds or wind. When you go home, look for signs of nature wherever you are.

HOT SPRINGS SAVE BISON

Yellowstone is in deep freeze! The temperature dropped to -60°F. That's bad news for bison.

Bison have great insulation. They have layers of fat, thick skin, and an undercoat of fur that is especially thick and soft. On top of all that, they have long coarse hairs that form a protective overcoat. But all this is not enough when temperatures dip, as they did today, below -30°F.

To make matters worse, Yellowstone gets as much as 50 feet of snow per year. Bison use their strong necks like snowplows, swinging side to side to push the snow away. But when the snow is almost as tall as they are, this gets too hard to do.

They have to go where it is warmer, or they may not survive.

The thermal river saves the day. The river does not freeze because the volcano beneath Yellowstone keeps the earth warm and sends hot steam and water into the river. The bison follow the river to the warm springs, where the snow gives way to grass below. Food at last!

But the bison cannot stay here for long because the grass has silica in it. Silica wears down their teeth. Warmer temperatures are predicted to arrive in the next few weeks. Soon the bison will be able to move on. In the meantime, the hot springs are a real bison-lifesaver.

BE SAFE! ALWAYS CHECK WITH PARK STAFF AND KEEP A SAFE DISTANCE FROM ANY WILD ANIMAL, INCLUDING BISON.

LEARN MORE

BOOKS

Del Grande, Stephanie. *Yellowstone National Park for Kids, Preteens, and Teenagers*. Lincoln, NE: iUniverse books.

Flynn, Sarah. *National Parks Guide U.S.A.*, Washington, D.C.: National Geographic. Buddy Bison appears 27 times throughout this book. Everyone can try to find Buddy while learning more about our national parks, including Yellowstone.

Frisch, Nate. *Yellowstone National Park*. Mankato, MN: Creative Paperback.

Knapp, Patty. *Getting to Know Yellowstone National Park*. Moose, WY: M.I. Adventure Publications.

Petersen, David. *Yellowstone National Park*. New York, NY: Children's Press.

WEBSITES

A note for parents and teachers: For more information on this topic, you can visit these websites with your young readers.

National Park Trust
parktrust.org/youthprograms/buddy-bison
Map and track where you have taken your Buddy Bison®.

Natgeo.com/kids/parks

National Park Service: Yellowstone
nps.gov/yell/learn/kidsyouth/index.htm

Smithsonian National Zoo
nationalzoo.si.edu/animals/american-bison

Staff for This Book
Erica Green, *Project Editor*
Julide Dengel, *Art Director and Designer*
Lisa Jewell, *Photo Editor*
Debbie Gibbons, *Director of Maps*
Paige Towler, *Editorial Assistant*
Sanjida Rashid and Rachel Kenny, *Design Production
    Assistants*
Michael McNey, *Map Research and Production*
Tammi Colleary-Loach, *Rights Clearance Manager*
Michael Cassady and Mari Robinson, *Rights Clearance
    Specialists*
Grace Hill, *Managing Editor*
Joan Gossett, *Senior Production Editor*
Lewis R. Bassford, *Production Manager*
Jennifer Hoff, *Manager, Production Services*
Susan Borke, *Legal and Business Affairs*

Senior Management Team, Kids Publishing and Media
Nancy Laties Feresten, *Senior Vice President*; Erica Green,
Vice President, *Editorial Director, Kids Books*; Julie
Vosburgh Agnone, *Vice President, Operations*; Jennifer
Emmett, *Vice President, Content*; Michelle Sullivan, *Vice
President, Video and Digital Initiatives*; Eva Absher-Schantz,
Vice President, Visual Identity; Rachel Buchholz, *Editor and
Vice President*, NG Kids magazine; Jay Sumner, *Photo
Director*; Hannah August, *Marketing Director*; R. Gary
Colbert, *Production Director*

Digital Laura Goertzel, *Manager*; Sara Zeglin, *Senior
Producer*; Bianca Bowman, *Assistant Producer*; Natalie
Jones, *Senior Product Manager*

**NATIONAL
PARK TRUST.**
TREASURE FOREVER.

Founded in 1983, National Park Trust, a 501(c)3 nonprofit, is
dedicated to preserving parks today and creating park
stewards for tomorrow. NPT has completed more than 100
land acquisition and preservation projects in 33 states and
Washington, D.C. Furthermore to address the growing
disconnect between kids and our parks, NPT initiated two
nationally recognized youth programs: the Buddy Bison School
Program and Kids to Parks Day, a national grassroots
movement celebrated annually on the 3rd Saturday in May.
To learn more, visit parktrust.org

T'S NO FUN TO BE A LONE WOLF!

e how a young wolf's confidence ws when he's nurtured by friendship.

Spring blooms over the Sawtooth Mountains of Idaho. Wildflowers splash patches of bright colors across the meadows. And a young wolf pup, Lakota, rolls in the fresh green grass.

Lakota spends all day playing. He turns every rock, log, and stick into a toy. His days are simple and fun.

But in a wolf's world, things can change quickly.

NATIONAL GEOGRAPHIC